D0575611
THIS BOOK IS A GIFT OF:
FRIENDS OF THE ORINDA LIBRARY
WITHDRAWN
CONTRA COSTA COUNTY LIBRARY

Claudia Mills
Pictures by **R. W. Alley**

Farrar, Straus and Giroux / New York

Distributed in Canada by Douglas & McIntyre Publishing Group
Color separations by Embassy Graphics
Printed and bound in the United States of America by
Phoenix Color Corporation
Designed by Barbara Grzeslo
First edition, 2005
1 3 5 7 9 10 8 6 4 2

www.fsgkidsbooks.com

Library of Congress Cataloging-in-Publication Data
Mills, Claudia.
Ziggy's blue-ribbon day / Claudia Mills ; pictures by R.W. Alley.— 1st ed.
p. cm.
Summary: Ziggy does not do well on the school track and field day events, but he feels much better after his classmates recognize his drawing talent.
ISBN-13: 978-0-374-32352-3
ISBN-10: 0-374-32352-6
[1. Track and field—Fiction. 2. Drawing—Fiction. 3. Contests—Fiction. 4. Self-esteem—Fiction. 5. Schools—Fiction.] I. Alley, R.W. (Robert W.), ill. II. Title.

PZ7.M63963Zi 2005
[E]—dc21

2003044057

For R. W. Alley, the artist Ziggy would want to grow up to be
—C.M.

For Claudia Mills, blue-ribbon writer
—R.W.A.

RUN
JUMP
THROW!

Ziggy hated track-and-field day.

He wasn't good at running races. He wasn't good at long jumping. He wasn't good at high jumping. He wasn't good at throwing balls.

Ziggy was good at sitting still and drawing pictures. But there was no picture-drawing event on track-and-field day.

“All right,” Mrs. Hanson said to her second-grade class that morning. “What are the three important things for us to do today?”

Janina waved her hand. “Do our best.”

Ziggy planned to do his best. But his best was worse than everyone else’s best. His best was worse than Janina’s worst.

Natalie spoke next. “Cheer for everybody.”

“Even if they come in last,” Kevin added.

Sally turned toward the boys.

“Even if they really stink!” Buster shouted, without raising his hand, as usual. Once, Buster told Ziggy that his running really stank.

Ziggy looked down at his desk. He had just finished drawing a castle with turrets and spires. Now he was starting a picture of a fire-breathing dragon.

"Nobody stinks, Buster," Mrs. Hanson said. "But you should definitely cheer for everyone."

Ziggy planned to cheer.

"There is one more important thing to do on track-and-field day," Mrs. Hanson said. "Does anyone know what it is?"

Ziggy couldn't imagine. Pray for rain, maybe?

"The most important thing to do on track-and-field day," Mrs. Hanson said, "is have fun!"

Well, at least Ziggy could do two out of three.

When it was time to go outdoors, Mrs. Hanson's students lined up, carrying their chairs. Taped to the back of every chair was an envelope. The envelope was to hold the ribbons won in each event.

There were four kinds of ribbons. Blue was best, then red, then gold, then silver. They called it silver, but it was really a dull, dismal gray. Ziggy knew he'd have an envelope full of gray ribbons at the end of the day.

At the last minute, Ziggy grabbed a handful of markers from his desk and crammed them into his pockets. Maybe he could decorate his envelope in between events. If it was going to have gray ribbons inside, it should be colorful outside.

TRACK
-AND-
FIELD
—DAY→

The spring day was beautiful, not too hot, not too cold. The sky was a bright blue. There were lots of fluffy white clouds, but not a single gray one. So much for praying for rain.

The opening event was the half-mile run—around the school field four times.

The girls ran first. Ziggy cheered them on. As he did, he drew a picture on his envelope of a castle *and* a dragon *and* a knight in shining armor. He could cheer and draw at the same time.

"Go, Janina!" he yelled. "Go, Sally! Go, Natalie!"

Janina won. She got a blue ribbon. Sally and Natalie came in close behind her. They got red ribbons. The girls who came in far behind them got gold ribbons. Finally came the girls who had to walk the last part of the race. They were red-faced and panting and close to tears. Gray ribbons.

That's my future, Ziggy thought.

The boys' turn came. Ziggy could hear the girls cheering. "Go, Kevin!" Kevin was the fastest runner of the boys. "Go, Buster!" Ziggy thought he heard Natalie shouting, "Go, Ziggy!"

But he couldn't go any faster. His side hurt too much. He couldn't breathe.

Ziggy finished the race red-faced and panting and close to tears.

"Here's your ribbon!" Mr. C., the P.E. teacher, handed him a gray ribbon. Of course.

"Nice race," Buster said to Ziggy. Ziggy knew Buster was teasing.

During the long jump, on his first try, Ziggy jumped too late. On his second try, he jumped too soon. Gray ribbon.

Janina and Natalie and Sally got blue ribbons. Kevin and Buster got reds.

During the high jump, Ziggy couldn't make himself jump at all. He ran up to the bar, and stopped.

"Try again, Ziggy!" Mr. C. encouraged him.

Ziggy ran up to the bar, and stopped.

"One last try!"

Ziggy ran up to the bar, and stopped. Another gray ribbon.

"Next!" Mr. C. called out.

During the softball throw, Buster threw the ball farthest of all. Ziggy threw the ball a long, long way, but it went high up into the air, instead of far out onto the field. It plopped down to earth by the gray-ribbon mark.

"Time for a water break!" Mr. C. called out.

NATALIE

At their seats, the children compared ribbons as Mrs. Hanson passed out water bottles.

"How many blue ribbons do you have?" Buster asked Ziggy.

Ziggy didn't answer.

Janina stared at Ziggy's decorated envelope. "Wow!" she said. "Your envelope is beautiful. Will you draw on mine for me?"

Ziggy hesitated. Did she really mean it?

"I'll give you one of my blue ribbons."

"Sure!"

Ziggy pulled out his markers and set to work. On Janina's envelope he drew a castle with a princess in it. He knew girls liked princesses.

Buster came back to his seat for another drink of water. "You sure don't stink at drawing," he told Ziggy. Buster held out a blue ribbon to Ziggy. "Will you do my envelope, too?"

Ziggy grinned at Buster.

Buster grinned back. "Put a huge dragon on mine," he commanded.

During the hoppy-ball race, Ziggy drew a huge dragon for Buster.

During the jump-rope race, he decorated Kevin's.

During the egg-on-a-spoon race, he decorated Natalie's.

SALLY
JANINA
NATALIE

When the races were over, Ziggy looked in his envelope. He had five blue ribbons! He knew they didn't really count as track-and-field-day blue ribbons. They weren't blue ribbons for running or jumping or throwing a ball. They were blue ribbons for doing what he loved to do.

Mrs. Hanson handed out Popsicles.

Ziggy tore off the paper and licked his. Nothing tasted better than a cool orange Popsicle at the end of track-and-field day, when you had done your best, cheered for others—and had fun, too.